# JAMES STEVENSON

# "Could Be Worse!"

MULBERRY BOOKS • New York

Printed in the United States of America.      First Mulberry Edition, 1987.      6  7  8  9  10

Library of Congress Cataloging in Publication Data
Stevenson, James  (date)  "Could be worse!"
Summary: Everything is always the same at Grandpa's house,
even the things he says—until one unusual morning.
[I.  Dreams—Fiction]  I.  Title.  PZ7.S84748Co  [E]
76-28534  ISBN 0-688-07035-3

# "Could Be Worse!"

At Grandpa's house things were always the same.

Grandpa always had the same thing for breakfast. Every day he read the paper.

And he always said the same thing.

No matter what.

One day Mary Ann said, "How come Grandpa never says anything interesting?"
"I guess it's because nothing interesting happens to him," said Louie.

Next morning at breakfast Grandpa said something different.
He said, "Guess what!

Last night, when I was asleep,

a large bird pulled me out of bed and took me for a long ride

and dropped me in the mountains.

I heard a noise. It was an abominable snowman with a huge snowball

which he threw at me.

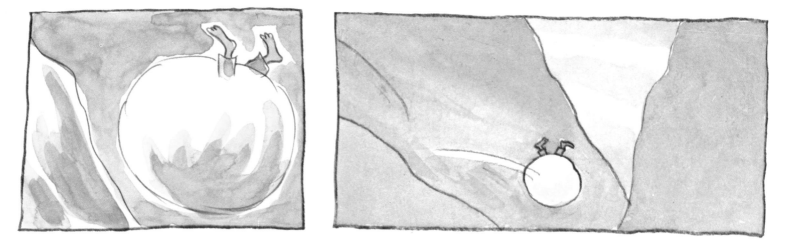

I got stuck inside the snowball, which rolled down the mountain.

It finally landed on the desert and began to melt.

I walked across the desert. Suddenly

I heard footsteps coming nearer and nearer.

A moment later I got squished by a giant something-or-other.

Before I could get up, I heard a strange noise.
A great blob of marmalade was coming toward me.

It chased me across the desert until . . .

I crashed into something tall. It was sort of like an ostrich and very cross.

It gave me a big kick. I went up into some storm clouds,

almost got hit by lightning, fell out of the clouds,

and landed in an ocean. I sank down about a mile to the bottom.

I saw an enormous goldfish coming at me.

I swam away as fast as I could and hid under a cup that had air in it.

When it was safe, I crawled out. I started to walk, but my foot got stuck

in the grip of a gigantic lobster.

I didn't know what to do. But just then a big squid came along

and squirted black ink all over the lobster. I escaped and

hitched a ride on a sea turtle that was going to the top for a bit of sunshine.
I was fortunate to find a piece of toast floating by and rode to shore,

where I discovered a newspaper. I quickly folded it into an airplane

and flew across the sea

and back home to bed.

Now, what do you think of that?"